For Max, Charlie and Patrick
A&C Guillain

PIRATE HIDEOUT

EGMONT
We bring stories to life

First published in Great Britain 2015 by Egmont UK Limited
This edition published in 2017
The Yellow Building, 1 Nicholas Road, London W11 4AN

www.egmont.co.uk

Text copyright © Adam and Charlotte Guillain 2015
Illustrations copyright © Lee Wildish 2015

The moral rights of the authors and illustrator have been asserted.

ISBN 978 1 4052 7361 9 (Paperback)

A CIP catalogue record for this title is available from the British Library.

PIZZA FOR PIRATES

Adam & Charlotte Guillain

Lee Wildish

EGMONT

A boy called George had a wonderful plan
To sail with a fine **pirate crew**.

So he packed up a **pizza**, his favourite feast,
And rowed off on the wide ocean blue.

George travelled for hours till he spotted dry land,

And saw mermaids on rocks from afar.

As he steered into port, he heard, "Pieces of eight!"

And a loud, croaky voice roaring,

"Arrrr!"

"Ahoy there!" cried George, and he held up his sword,
"Please can I be a PIRATE like you?"

But all he heard was a flap and a screech . . .

...then a **noisy bird** burst into view!

"I'm a **parrot!**" it squawked, as it perched on his head,
"And pirates love parrots, I'm told.
I'll help you to track down a whole pirate crew,
And we'll find **treasure chests** full of gold."

George steered his boat on through the choppy green waves,
As a **shiver of sharks** glided by.

Then he spotted a shape in the mist up ahead,
So he popped a **patch** over his eye.

"Is it a **pirate ship**?" George asked the bird.
The parrot screeched, "Where is its sail?"

George peered through the telescope and gave a cry . . .

"That's no pirate ship!
Look - it's a **whale!**"

They tried to escape
from the whale's gaping mouth,
But a wave swept the boat in its **jaws!**

With a whoosh, George was swallowed.

How would he escape?

He'd even lost one of his oars!

George switched on his torch and he looked all about,

While the parrot flew down with a flap.

"Shiver me timbers!" cried George when he saw

A hat and an old treasure map.

As he put on the pirate hat, George told the bird,

"Get back in the boat, I've a plan!

Think of the best pirate joke that you know,

And then squawk it as loud as you can!"

When the bird told the joke,

a strange sound could be heard -
First a **rumble** and then a **loud roar!**

"The whale's laughing!" said George, with a sigh of relief,

Then he paddled like mad with his oar.

They shot out of the mouth of the chuckling whale,
And splashed through the waves and the spray,

Till the parrot called out, "Land ahoy, George me lad!"
And they steered the boat into a bay.

George stepped on to the sand, then he crept up the beach,
While above him his parrot friend flew.

At the sound of loud voices, he peered through the trees,
And saw there . . .

...a real **pirate** crew!

"Avast there, me hearties!" called George with a wave,

"Please can I be a pirate, like you?"

Then he held out a dripping wet box and announced,

"I brought **pizza** for the whole crew!"

The Captain squirmed, "Matey, you seem a fine lad,
But that thing you call pizza looks YUCK!"

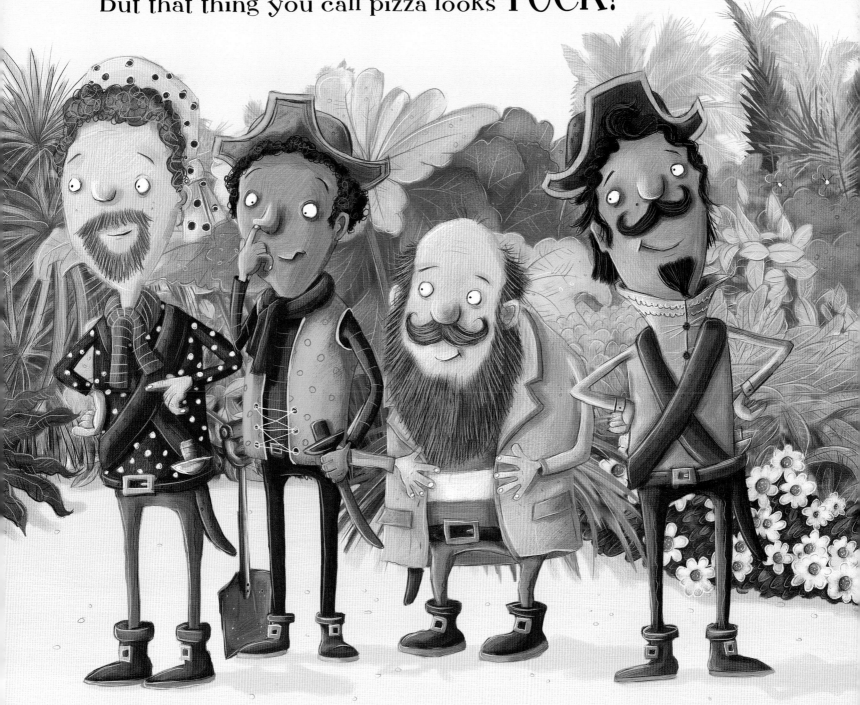

Then he gasped as he stared down at George's wet head,
"You've found my best hat - we're in luck!"

"Is my **treasure map** with it?" the Captain asked George,

"I lost them both long, long ago."

"Yes, it is!" exclaimed George, and he held up the map,

Then he read it and shouted, "Let's go!"

They walked this way and that, till George came to a stop,
"It's here," he said, "Dig! No one rest!"
The shipmates worked hard in the burning hot sun,
Till they'd dug up . . .

...a huge **treasure** chest!

But while the pirates grabbed handfuls of gold
A green tentacle crept up the beach!

Then a **sea monster** suddenly burst from the depths,
And carried the chest out of reach!

It lifted the treasure towards its huge mouth,
George shouted, "Stop! Listen to me!
Eat this **pizza** instead, you can have the whole thing,
It's much tastier than treasure, you'll see!"

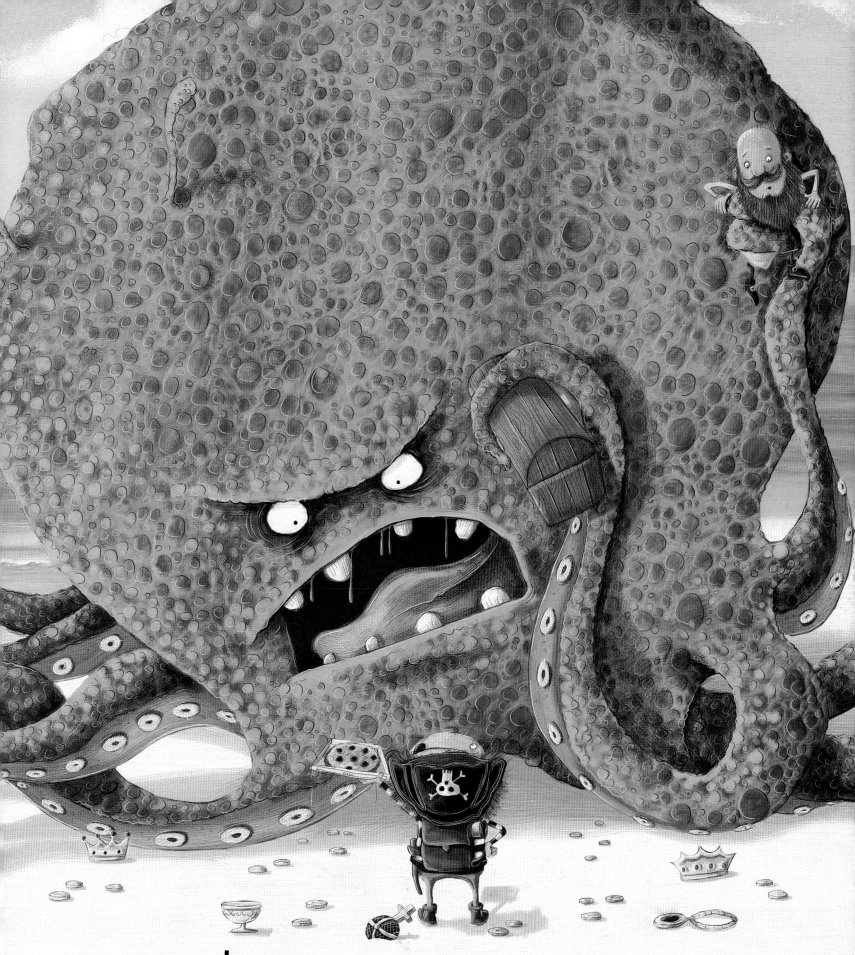

The **monster** glared down at the dripping wet snack . . .

Then it **gobbled** it up in one bite!

It put down the chest and the crew roared, "George lad,

You're the **best kind of pirate**, all right!"

Then the Captain said, "George, now you're one of the crew,
There is just one more thing to be done.

We must head for our ship and then
you'll **walk the plank** ...

And we'll show you how **pirates have fun!**"